KV-191-973

Dragon Dramatics

Dragon Dramatics

Jonathan Allen

ORCHARD BOOKS

540962

MORAY DISTRICT COUNCIL

DEPARTMENT OF

LEISURE AND LIBRARIES

JB

ORCHARD BOOKS

96 Leonard Street, London EC2A 4RH

Orchard Books Australia

14 Mars Road, Lane Cove, NSW 2066

ISBN 1 85213 888 2

First published in Great Britain in 1995

Copyright © Jonathan Allen 1995

The right of Jonathan Allen to be identified as the author and
illustrator of this work has been asserted by him in accordance
with the Copyright, Designs and Patents Act, 1988.
A CIP catalogue record for this book is available from
the British Library.
Printed in Great Britain

Contents

Enter the
Dragon

A long time ago, as many of you will know already, there lived a very famous wizard called Grimweed. He was mostly famous for his potions, but he was a wizard of many parts as they say, and certainly knew his way round a magic wand and a spell book. Such was his skill and talent that,

as well as being voted number one in the Wiz Biz for the thirteenth year running at the three Ws annual conference, he was given a special All Round Wizard Award for Services to Magic. He was quite amused by the title. Not least because with his cloak and his pointy hat he looked anything but 'all round' in fact he was positively triangular. But, despite all the praise coming his way, Grimweed was not one to let it go to his head. Well, perhaps every now and then he might have mentioned it to one or two people, and he may have had it put on a sign outside Magic City in magic Day-Glo letters, but he was, by and large, quite a modest wizard.

People came to Grimweed from far and wide with all sorts of problems. Most of these problems, even the more complicated ones, could usually be cured by the simple application of the correct potion. To this end Grimweed had set up a While-U-Wait potion service, where highly trained staff could deal with the straightforward cases while the more complicated, and therefore more interesting cases, were sent straight through to his special consulting room. This story concerns one of these more complicated problems but, funnily enough, it didn't get quite as far as Grimweed's consulting room.

It was the sight of a dragon turning in at his front gate that snapped Grimweed out of his daydream. He stared at it for a moment in disbelief then pulling himself together, jumped to his feet and hurried over to the window to get a better view. He gave a low whistle. What a dragon! It was over ten metres long, and its whole body, from the end of its nose right down to the tip of its magnificent tail, was covered in bright red scales. Its huge wings were

folded tight against its back and, as Grimweed watched, a wisp of smoke curled upwards from its nostrils. This was the real thing all right.

About five metres in front of the dragon trudged a man, a bedraggled, tired-looking man carrying a knapsack and wearing what can best be described as a hunted expression. It wasn't as if he was unaware of the dragon behind him, he seemed all too aware of it and you could tell that it didn't exactly make his day. As he made his way up the drive the dragon

followed at a discreet distance, all the while looking at the man's back with the kind of expression more likely to be found on the face of a spaniel of strictly limited intelligence who wants his tummy tickled.

As Grimweed took in this scene he noticed that Lloyd, his assistant, had joined him and was standing at his side, eyes shining. Lloyd looked at Grimweed.

"A dragon!" he breathed. "A real dragon! I've never seen one before. Isn't it the most fabulous thing you've ever seen?"

Grimweed smiled a secret smile. He was remembering *his* first sight of a dragon. Not a recent event, but still as fresh in his mind as if it had happened yesterday . . .

"It's a Throolian Red," said Grimweed, in a hushed voice, "a female, about one hundred and ten years old, give or take a decade, so she's still a youngster, and yes, she's a beauty!"

In the shrubbery half-concealed potion customers who had taken refuge there at the dragon's first appearance were peering anxiously out, wondering what would happen. Noticing this, Grimweed squared his shoulders and stepped forward.

"Come on, Lloyd," he said briskly, "Let's go and see what this is all about!"

"Er, is it safe?" asked Lloyd, looking rather doubtful.

" Safe? Of course it's safe!" said Grimweed, "Don't be silly. It's only a dragon."

Wings of
Desire

"Hello, and welcome to Magic City!" cried Grimweed, shaking the man's hand. "My name's Grimweed, and this is my assistant, Lloyd. Come on in and tell us what the problem is, and, er, bring your friend."

"Some friend!" groaned the man.

The dragon waggled its tail in a friendly kind of way, and blew a delicate wisp of smoke from its left nostril.

"This dragon," the man continued, "has been following me around night and day for the last month!"

"Wow!" gasped Lloyd, "Lucky you!"

"Lucky!" snorted the man. "You try running a successful business when your customers are scared off by the sight of a huge red dragon leering at them through the shop window!" He shook his head. "My name's Crump, by the way, Horatio Crump of Crump's Cleverly Crafted Chocolate Confection Company, of Flooing City. Pleased to meet you."

"Likewise, Mr Crump, likewise!" said Grimweed with enthusiasm. I know the name well. I myself am particularly partial to your chocolate-covered toffee twists. The best in the kingdom in my opinion."

"Thank you," said Mr Crump, bowing.

"Well, if you would be good enough to come with me," Grimweed continued, "we can discuss your interesting problem in a bit more comfort."

While Lloyd arranged some chairs in the courtyard (the dragon wouldn't have fitted in the consulting room), Grimweed went inside to look for something. Lloyd and Mr Crump sat down. The dragon lay on the ground a few metres away and watched them with interest.

"She's not your dragon then?" said Lloyd, returning the dragon's gaze.

"No she's not my dragon!" cried Mr Crump. "She seems to *think* she's my dragon but she's not! I wish whoever's dragon she *is* would come and take her away. I'm absolutely fed up with dragons and everything to do with them!"

"I'm sorry to hear that," said Grimweed, stepping back into the courtyard, "but you'll be pleased to know that I've got one or two ideas about her ownership, if you can call it that, but first" – he bent down and grinned at the dragon– "Daddy's got something for you!"

He stuck out his hand. On his palm was a large green biscuit shaped like a star. The dragon regarded it with considerable interest. As Grimweed jiggled the biscuit

around in his hand the dragon waggled her tail and heaved herself up.

"That's right," cooed Grimweed, "snacky-poos! Come on girl, come and get it!"

The dragon stuck out her tongue, and licked the edge of her mouth (dragons don't have lips.)

"It's a Grimproductz Dragon Krunchee-Snak Biscuit," Grimweed explained to Lloyd and Mr Crump, "Dragons love 'em."

He stood up, raised his arm in the air,

palm towards the dragon, and recited a little rhyme.

"Here's the hand, here's the biscuit.
Open your mouth, or daren't you risk it?"

The dragon shuffled her feet and then, to Lloyd and Mr Crumps' astonishment, meekly opened her huge jaws, revealing a more than impressive set of teeth. They were the kind of teeth you'd like to have if you were considering biting trees in half.

Grimweed lobbed the biscuit into the dragon's mouth and backed away, pulling a face and wafting the air with his hat. The dragon's teeth may have been wonderful, but her breath wasn't – it smelt diabolical!

"With breath that bad I'm surprised dragons need to breathe fire!" gasped Mr Crump, "Yuk!"

"Grimweed! You've done that before, haven't you?" burst out Lloyd when he'd finished coughing. "Come on, out with it!"

"Once or twice," admitted Grimweed modestly. "It's the hand gestures that are important. What you say doesn't really matter, but Dragonmasters like to ham it up a bit, so I did."

"Dragonmasters!" cried Lloyd. "You're not telling me that you're a Dragonmaster as well as everything else, are you? I was wondering how come you knew so much about dragons."

"Well," said Grimweed, "I'm only a Bronze Wing and it was a long time ago, but yes, I am a Dragonmaster!"

"But," he continued, sitting down, "this is not getting us anywhere! Mr Crump, I think we should hear your story."

Mr Crump sighed.

"There's not much to tell," he began, "It's pretty straightforward really. One day when I was setting up the chocolate display stand outside my shop, the sky went dark and a great gust of wind blew my Fudge Centre Supremes all over the pavement. I was down on my hands and knees, picking them up, when I noticed that I was not alone. I looked round and got the shock of my life! A huge red dragon was sitting on the pavement not five metres from me, gulping down my chocolates like there was no tomorrow!"

"Wow!" gasped Lloyd, "I didn't know dragons liked chocolate!"

"Take it from me," said Mr Crump, "they do! Or at least this one does. Anyway," he went on, "as I crouched there, rooted to the spot with fear, I realised that the dragon was far more interested in chocolates than it was in me. So, gathering all my courage, I made a dash for the shop, threw myself in and locked the door!"

"So what did she do?" asked Grimweed. "Just hang around outside your shop waiting to be fed chocolate?"

"Yes," said Mr Crump, "except once when I tried to get away. I thought I'd escaped until I looked up and found that I was being tracked from the air. I was trapped! The dragon wouldn't go away as

long as I kept feeding her chocolates, but I couldn't risk stopping in case she decided to eat me instead!"

"Did she eat a lot of chocolate?" asked Grimweed, "or just the odd pound or two?"

"You must be joking!" cried Mr Crump, "She ate huge amounts of the stuff. I've been making five kilos a day just to keep her happy!"

"Hmmm, no wonder her breath smells!" muttered Grimweed. "Tell me, has she breathed any fire at all in the time you've known her, so to speak?"

"No, thank goodness," replied Mr Crump. "That would just about put the tin lid on it, burning my shop down too!"

"Sounds like her jets are blocked," said Grimweed to himself. "I'll see if I can sort out some dragon tonic later." He scratched his chin. "So you decided to come to me," he concluded. "A very wise decision, if I do say so myself."

Mr Crump shrugged.

"It didn't take much intelligence to see that it couldn't go on forever," he said.

"What would have happened when I ran out of chocolate for instance? It didn't bear thinking about. Right, I thought, dragons are magical creatures, or at least that's what people say, so maybe a wizard would know what to do. And who's the best wizard in these parts? Grimweed! So here I am."

"Well," said Grimweed, folding his arms, "You came to the right place, because I know exactly where this dragon comes from, and I know exactly how to get her back there too!"

Home Sweet Home?

The back of a flying dragon is a fascinating place to be. Lloyd certainly thought so. He gazed about him in wonder. It was hard to believe he wasn't dreaming.

Six hundred feet in the air is also a fascinating place to be, Mr Crump couldn't deny it, but all the same he would rather have been somewhere less fascinating – a lot less fascinating. He clung on to his Three Ws Approved Dragon Safety Harness, shut his eyes and groaned.

Grimweed had told him that because the dragon was a Throolian Red, and obviously a show dragon, it meant that she was almost definitely a refugee from the dragon stable of Gorgaz the Strong, King Dragonmaster, Lord of the Air! All that needed to be done was fly the dragon back to Castle Gorgaz, her home.

"Oh, is that all?" Mr Crump had said sarcastically. But no one had been listening. He hadn't wanted to come, but there wasn't much choice, the dragon wouldn't take off without him or his bag of chocolates, even though they were well past their sell-by date. He'd had to fight down his terror and climb on board. As Grimweed had pointed out, it was either that or being followed around by a dragon for the rest of his life. So here he was.

"Dragons have a strong homing instinct," Grimweed was explaining to Lloyd from his place between the dragon's wings. "Give them the command *Home!* and they don't stop until they get there. Which in our case, if I'm right, is Gorgaz the Strong's castle, way up in the Grutz Mountains."

"How long will it take?" Lloyd asked, watching the steady beat of the dragon's wings as she powered them through the air.

"About eight hours," said Grimweed, "It gets a bit boring at times, but its got to be one of the classiest ways to travel there is!"

"Who is this Gorgaz the Strong?" asked Mr Crump, trying not to look down. "He sounds like a pretty formidable character."

"Oh he is, he is," said Grimweed with a grin. "My old mate Quentin is seriously formidable!"

"What do you mean, your old mate, Quentin?" asked Lloyd, "do you know this person?"

Grimweed smiled.

"I was at Magic School with a small unassuming lad with the unfortunate name of Quentin Tinklebottom. We did our Basic Dragon Keeping course together. We were both good, but he seemed to have a natural feel for dragons. He got his Bronze Wings while I was only on my Intermediate Certificate he was that good. Anyway, to cut a long story short, he became a top Dragonmaster, while I moved on to potions, which suited me better. I haven't seen him for years, but we still keep in touch. And this dragon has all the hallmarks of his set-up to me."

"I can understand why he changed his name," said Lloyd, "but isn't Lord of the Air a bit over the top?"

"Oh, Dragonmasters have to be flamboyant," said Grimweed. "People expect it. It goes with the job really."

"What exactly is the job then?" asked Mr Crump, "I don't know much about dragons, despite having been closer to one than most people."

"Oh, it's a fascinating job!" enthused Grimweed. "They put on spectacular shows for special royal occasions. Quentin's aerial display team of Grutzian Blues is something to see! He has to dress up and look fierce because that's what people expect of him. He stands there making dramatic gestures and producing thunderous noises and huge flashes with his wand, while the dragons whoosh overhead breathing jets of flame and roaring. It's quite a show."

"Wow!" breathed Lloyd.

"The other popular job for trained dragons," continued Grimweed, "is pretending to be defeated in single combat by princes who are after the beautiful princess's hand in marriage, not to mention half the kingdom. Quentin does a good line in Guaranteed-to-Run-Away Fighting Dragons."

"What a good idea," mused Mr Crump. "If I was prince, I'd definitely hire one of those!"

"Actually, it's usually the princesses who hire them," added Grimweed. "Princesses don't like the idea of their boyfriends being eaten, or burned to a crisp, just for the sake of tradition. So they hire a trained dragon. It makes perfect sense."

"Doesn't it," agreed Lloyd, leaning back and watching the landscape slip by beneath them.

Grimweed, who was a comparatively seasoned dragon traveller, settled himself down and began to doze. Mr Crump tried to do likewise, but it wasn't easy.

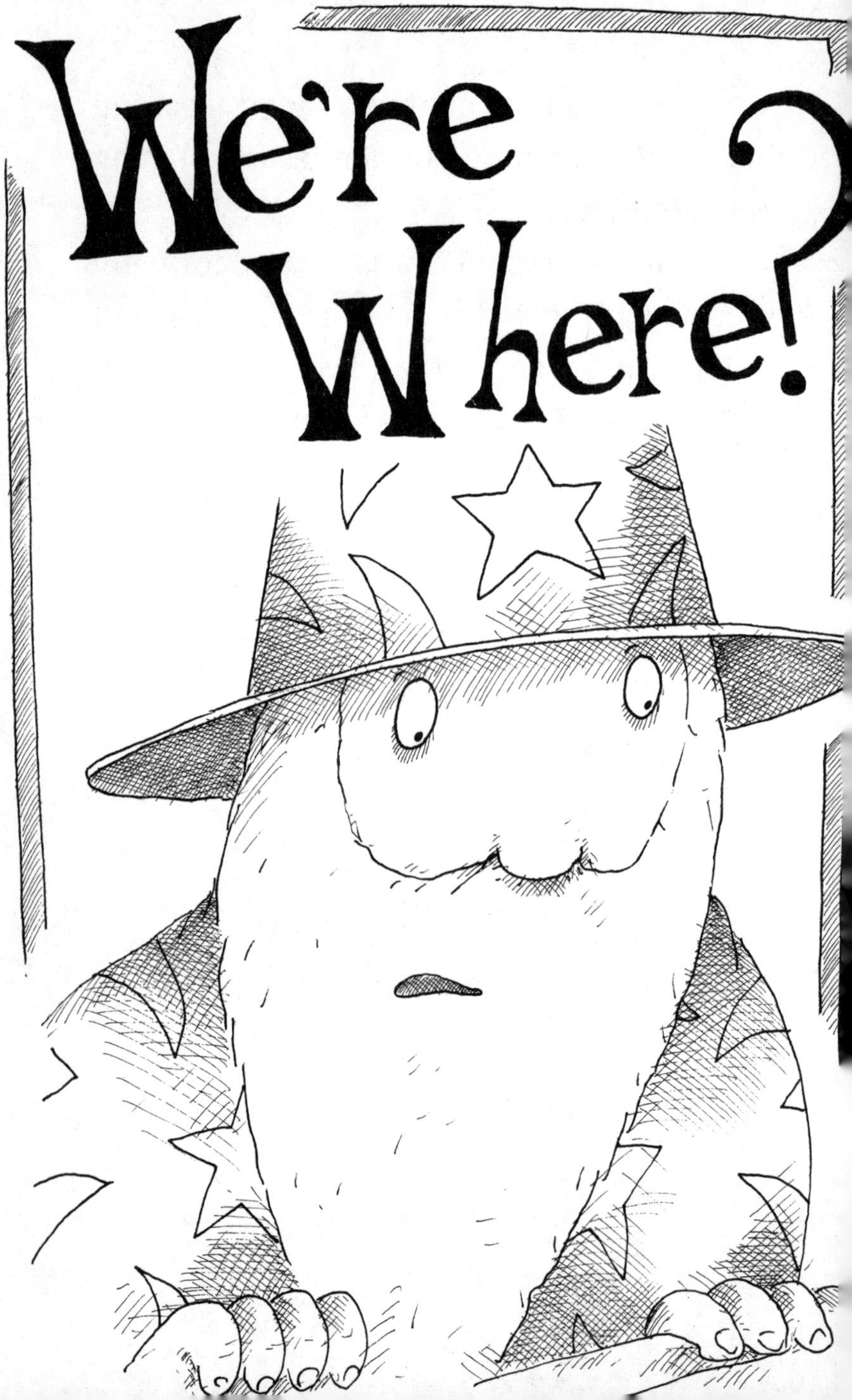
We're Where? Where!

After a couple of hours of steady if uneventful progress, Lloyd noticed that they were beginning to lose height. He watched carefully. Yes, the dragon was flying lower than a moment ago and was still descending. He didn't know where they were, but he could tell it wasn't the Grutz Mountains, unless someone had flattened them and then built a large number of houses. No, they were flying over a town. He leaned forward and shook Grimweed gently.

"Grimweed!" he hissed, "I don't want to alarm you, but we're coming down, and it's not where we're supposed to be coming down!"

"A wha. . . ?" spluttered Grimweed, waking up in confusion as Lloyd's message sank in. "Where are we?"

"I've no idea," said Lloyd, "but I know where we're not."

"Good heavens!" cried Mr Crump, who had woken up at the sound of Lloyd's voice, and was peering down at the streets below. "If I'm not mistaken it's Flooing City! And look! We're heading for my shop!"

"Uh, oh!" groaned Grimweed, "problem time!"

Sure enough the dragon was gliding down to a row of shops on a small street near the centre of town. People were pointing agitatedly and running. Doors were slamming and small children were being scooped up and carried indoors. Grimweed shook his head.

"This isn't your home, you daft dragon!"

The dragon made a perfect landing on the street outside Mr Crump's shop, and as there was nothing much else they could do, everybody got off and went inside.

"I know it's not a helpful thing to say, but I'm glad to be home!" said Mr Crump, putting the kettle on.

"Hmmm," said Grimweed gloomily, as he slumped into an armchair. "What I can't understand," he complained, "is how a dragon's homing instinct can be relocated, so to speak. I mean home is

41

home. It doesn't just shift for no good reason. I wish I had my Dragon Keeper's Bible here!"

"You're saying that the dragon came here instead of Quentin's place because, for reasons as yet undiscovered, her instinct is telling her that *this* is her home?" asked Lloyd, trying to get it clear in his own mind.

"More or less," said Grimweed, "but the question is, what are we going to do about it?"

"Couldn't you call this Gorgaz character and see if he's got any ideas?" suggested Lloyd. "You brought your Grimproductz Lightweight Traveller's Crystal Ball with you, didn't you?"

"Good thinking!" said Grimweed, rummaging in his travelling bag. "Good thinking! Ah, here it is."

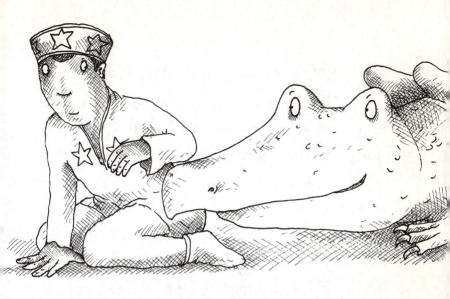

So while Grimweed contacted Quentin, alias Gorgaz the Strong (crystal balls work a bit like telephones), Lloyd amused himself outside by getting to know the dragon a bit better. He fed her some stale chocolates that Mr Crump had found in his knapsack. Then he scratched her snout with a stick, which proved popular. He was in the middle of trying to teach her to flick chocolates into her mouth with the end of her tail when Grimweed stuck his head round the door.

"Ok, let's get going!" he cried.

"Eh?" said Lloyd. "But won't we just end up back here again? What about the dodgy homing instinct?"

"Well, according to my recently received information," said Grimweed, "there's a kind of magical override, so you can switch off the homing instinct if you know the right magic word. Then you can steer the dragon by giving it instructions to go right or left, etc. It's easy, apparently." He clapped his hands. "Come on, what are you waiting for?"

The journey to Gorgaz the Strong's castle was uneventful. The magic override worked perfectly, and although Mr Crump had been reluctant to get back on board, he knew he didn't have much choice. Once they got to Quentin's place, Grimweed assured him, they would be able to sort things out once and for all. Mr Crump hoped he was right. When the spiky towers of Castle Gorgaz came into view at long last, he heaved a sigh of relief.

Lloyd was in a state of high excitement. He had just noticed a flock of smaller dragons zooming up towards them. Daisy had noticed them too. (Daisy was the missing dragon's name, Grimweed

had discovered.) She gave a kind of honk, and blew out a cloud of smoke.

"Steady now, girl!" said Grimweed in a calm voice. "There'll be plenty of time to play with your friends later."

They began to descend towards the dragon landing-strip now visible on the south tower, while around them, the smaller dragons dived and soared, blowing excited little darts of flame. As Daisy landed, Quentin and some of his more junior dragon handlers rushed forward.

"Daisy!" cried Quentin in excitement and threw his arms around the dragon's snout, then added, "you wicked girl! What do you mean by running off like that?"

Daisy gave a honk and blew out a cloud of smoke.

"Phew! She's got disgusting bad breath!" cried Quentin, pulling a face.

"Her jets are blocked," said Grimweed. "She hasn't breathed fire in the last month as far as I'm aware. Too much chocolate."

"Chocolate?" said Quentin, puzzled. "Since when have dragons eaten that?"

"Well," said Grimweed, climbing down from Daisy's back, "combine that with the misplaced homing instinct, and it has to add up to something significant. I've been trying to work it out all the way here. I've got a vague idea, but I need to look something up in your Dragonkeeper's Bible. "

"Go ahead," said Quentin, "and while you're busy doing that I'll give Daisy some of that excellent dragon tonic you sent me last year. There's still some left. You'll find the book in my study."

"Any luck?" asked Quentin as he stuck his head round the study door ten minutes later. "I've given her the tonic, and my assistants are checking her over. She should be back to normal in no time. "

"I wouldn't be so sure," said Grimweed with a grin. "Oh, it's all right, Quentin," he added when he saw the worried expression on Quentin's face, "there's nothing actually *wrong* with her. Look, I'll give you a clue. You know when a female dragon reaches a certain age, her thoughts turn to, er, shall we say, *other things*?"

Quentin looked at him, puzzled. Then his jaw dropped.

"She's not!" he gasped "you don't think she's . . . she's . . . PREGNANT?" He slid into the nearest armchair. "How come I never noticed? I must have been so busy getting her ready for the King of Malvolia's show that I just didn't see it! Not that it's easy to spot at the best of times."

"In your book," said Grimweed, "it says that dragons are a bit like humans when they are pregnant, in that they develop cravings for unusual foods. And it also says that in a very few cases the homing instinct, and other direction-finding mechanisms can be upset."

Quentin shook his head. He looked shocked, but not displeased.

"Er, can someone explain this to me?" requested Mr Crump who had followed Quentin into the study. "Does this mean that once she's had her babies she'll be back to normal and stop following me around?"

"Yes," said Grimweed simply. " What I think has happened is this. Being pregnant has messed around with her natural functions, not to get too technical. In Daisy's case her homing instinct was affected and she got lost. Her craving for chocolate led her to your shop, and once there, her homing instinct got kind of locked in. So she hung around because all her instincts were telling her that it was her home. She followed you around because, as you were the one feeding her, she figured you must be her master."

"I can see you have an interesting story to tell me," said Quentin to Mr Crump, "but it will have to wait, I'm afraid. Daisy is going to need some special attention!"

"And sooner than you think!" put in Grimweed. He'd just caught a fleeting glimpse of one of Quentin's dragon handlers dashing past the window towards the study door, face red with exertion. The door burst open and the handler rushed in.

"It's Daisy!" she cried, "something's wrong!"

"It's all right, Tabitha," said Quentin reassuringly. "I know what it is, and I'll be right there! Grimweed, Lloyd, I'll need your help!"

If you've never seen a baby dragon you've missed something really very special. Baby dragons are like miniature versions of adult dragons only less pointy somehow. They don't have teeth for the first three months, and their wings are barely more than flaps for the first six, but each scale is perfectly formed. They're not green or red, like their parents, they're a beautiful bright yellow.

Grimweed, Lloyd, and even Mr Crump were captivated by the little creatures as they watched them playing around their mother's feet.

"Are they sweet, or what?" said Lloyd.

"Well done, Daisy!" said Mr Crump, "I wouldn't have been so nasty about you if I'd known what it was all about."

Mr Crump, Grimweed and Lloyd stayed on at Quentin's castle for the next two weeks, partly because then they could hitch a lift home on the big transport dragon that would be carrying the equipment for the King of Malvolia's show, and partly because they were having such a good time. Lloyd was in seventh heaven. Quentin had got his daughter Jade to show him round the dragon pens, and had let him help in the preparations for the show. He was a natural. He loved the dragons and the dragons loved him. Not only that, Jade had taken quite a liking to him as well.

Mr Crump had found the kitchens, and was busily engaged in swapping recipes with the castle chef, who was turning out to be no mean chocolate maker. Grimweed spent his time watching Quentin rehearse his dragons for the big show and talking over old times with him in front of a roaring fire. Quentin's other daughter, Grace, was very interested in potions and spent many hours quizzing Grimweed and talking over her ideas with him. He was very impressed by her grasp of the subject. So it came as no surprise when Lloyd, Jade and Grace approached him the day before they were due to leave.

"Er, ahem!" coughed Lloyd nervously. "Er, um, I've been thinking. I've really enjoyed being here and learning about dragons, and, er, basically I want to stay and study for my Bronze Wings!"

"Uh huh?" said Grimweed, raising one eyebrow.

"And I want to come with you and study potions at Magic City!" put in Grace. "I've asked Dad and he says it's all right with him but that it's your decision. I could do a swap with Lloyd!" she added brightly.

"Uh huh," said Grimweed again. "You're both deadly serious about this?" he asked.

"Absolutely!" they replied together.

"Well," said Grimweed, "Lloyd, I can spare you for six months, which should give you time to get your wings, but you'll have to come back and do your silver leaves exam for your potions diploma. After that you can decide what you want to do. A wizard must follow his own path." Lloyd grinned. "And, Grace," Grimweed continued, "I'd be delighted to take you on for the same period. It'll be hard work, but I think you'll enjoy it."

Grace gave an excited gasp and ran off to tell her dad.

Grimweed helped Mr Crump off the transport dragon and into his shop. They were dropping him off on the way back to Magic City.

"Before I say goodbye," said Grimweed, "and by way of compensation for your trouble and your lost business, I've run you up a little something." He reached into the pocket of his robe and brought out a small bottle, and a neat little box.

"It was Quentin's idea," he added. "Go on, open it."

Inside the box was a perfectly crafted mould in the shape of a dragon. Mr Crump gasped in admiration .

"What a wonderful idea!" he breathed.

"And if you're not offended by the idea," Grimweed carried on, "I invented a potion just for you. It's called Choc-Perfecto potion, and it makes chocolate just the right consistency for making chocolate dragons from moulds such as the one you're holding."

"Ooh!" said Mr Crump, "Thank you! I'm not offended – it will be extremely useful. I mean I don't want to lose any of this fine detail, do I?"

"Oh yes, and before I forget –" Grimweed reached into his pocket, " – here's a small can of Grimproductz Dragon Repellent spray! You never know when it might come in useful!"

Mr Crump laughed.

"Well," Grimweed grinned, "I can't solve problems without getting a couple of potions in *somewhere*, can I? I've got my reputation to think of!"

GRIMFAX

I suppose it's accurate to describe dragons as magical creatures – they are to us – but in Grimweed's time they were as real as you or me, or Mrs Johnson down the road. (Especially Mrs Johnson down the road).

That aside, there were actually some real magical creatures around. Warlock Wolloonboot was very interested in Wolf Magic and was responsible for the first Where Wolf. This was a half man, half wolf creature that roamed the forests on moonlit nights. It was called a Where Wolf for the same reason that it roamed the forest – it didn't know where it was. The Where Wolf developed a habit of jumping out in front of travellers, baring its fangs, then asking the way to Blongville, or wherever, and enquiring if it could borrow a road map.

Warlock Wolloonboot also came up with the What Wolf (it was invisible), the When Wolf (it never turned up), and the more useful How Wolf. The How wolf would roam the forests at night, giving unwary travellers D.I.Y. tips and advising them on the best tiime to water their gooseberries. But before he could develop a Why Wolf or even a Who Wolf, a party of disgruntled traveller's chased him out of town, and a good thing it was too.

Oh well, I haven't got time to tell you about the Fairy Dogmother, or the Unique Horn, so they will just have to wait for another time.

Johnathan Allen lives in Hertfordshire with his wife, Marian, their small daughter, Isobel, and his cat, William. When not writing or drawing, he likes eating, birdwatching, listening to and playing music.

BEST WISHES . . . . .

This book encourages the growing intelligence of the young child . . .

it stimulates thought, strengthens memory and encourages the use of language.

The recognition and interpretation of the pictures and situations lead to enquiry, observation of detail, the realization of how things relate to one another, the making of inferences and the forming of conclusions and judgments.

As progress is made through the book, the child adds to his store of general knowledge and how to apply it to new situations. Confidence grows with a fuller understanding of the complex life around.

The use of this book should form a part of any pre-reading programme.

This book has been specially planned to be enjoyed *with* your children.

They should be encouraged to talk freely about each picture, perhaps recalling their own experiences or possessions and relating them to the illustrations.

Do not hesitate to make any contribution which will encourage conversation.